STO

This book belongs to:

_____

D1307353

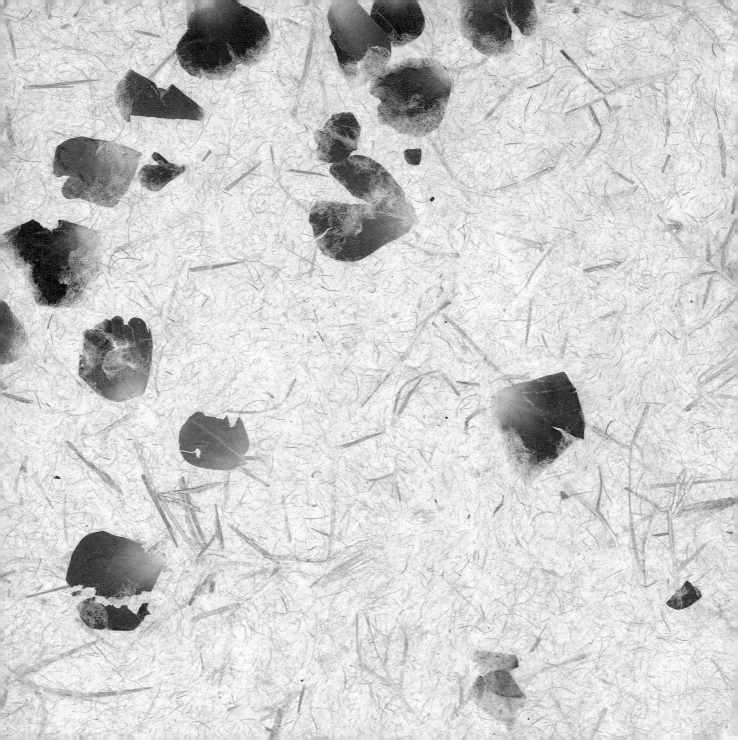

Pearl Plants a Tree

ALLEN COUNTY PUBLIC LIBRARY
CHILDREN'S SERVICES
P.O. BOX 2270
FORT WAYNE, INDIANA 46801

**kits
for
kids**

The purchase of this book
was made possible
through a joint effort of
Community Action of Northeast Indiana (CANI)
Allen County Public Library (ACPL)
and
The Step Ahead Council of Allen County

Pearl Plants a Tree

STORY AND PICTURES BY
JANE BRESKIN ZALBEN

SIMON & SCHUSTER
BOOKS FOR YOUNG READERS

Allen County Public Library
900 Webster Street
PO Box 2270
Fort Wayne, IN 46801-2270

*I wish to acknowledge my husband, Steven, "the Yeshiva bocher";
Rabbi Beth Davidson, whose help was invaluable; Rabbi Michael Klayman,
for making sure everything was "kosher"; my editor, Stephanie Owens Lurie,
for her honesty and advice; and Carol Roeder, for her marketing know-how
and friendship, once again. And all the Los Angeles librarians who have
been suggesting this for years.*

SIMON & SCHUSTER BOOKS FOR YOUNG READERS
An imprint of Simon & Schuster Children's Publishing Division
1230 Avenue of the Americas, New York, New York 10020
Copyright © 1995 by Jane Breskin Zalben
All rights reserved including the right of reproduction
in whole or in part in any form.
SIMON & SCHUSTER BOOKS FOR YOUNG READERS
is a trademark of Simon & Schuster.
Manufactured in the United States of America
10 9 8 7 6 5 4 3 2 1

Library of Congress Cataloging-in-Publication Data
Zalben, Jane Breskin.
Pearl plants a tree / story and pictures by Jane Breskin Zalben.   p.   cm.
Summary: In the spring Pearl and Grandpa plant an apple tree.
Discusses the celebration of Tu b'Shvat and other tree-planting
festivals around the world.
ISBN 0-689-80034-7
[1. Trees—Fiction.   2. Grandfathers—Fiction.]   I. Title.
PZ7.Z254Pd   1995   [E]—dc20   94-38404

To my mama,
Mae (Mindel) Kirshbloom Breskin,
from Bialystok to Borough Park and on,
and to my children,
and someday theirs.

*P*earl's grandpa took her back to the
old neighborhood and memories of
his first spring in America.
"This is the first house I lived in after
I came over on the boat from the old
country. The front stoop is so small.
I remember it *much* bigger," Grandpa said.
"There is the apple tree I planted from a seed.
That's where I had my first birthday party,
and where I asked Grandma to marry me.
I remember it *much* smaller."
That gave Pearl an idea.

When she got home, she took a seed from
her little brother Avi's apple, and planted it.

She put the pot on her windowsill.
She watered the seed. And waited.

Pearl dreamed of flowers and fruit
that grew and grew and became a
forest of light and air and leaves.

Pearl would hide and climb in the trees
and roll on the mossy hills below.
Or sometimes she might read quietly.

But now it was January. Cold.
And she longed for spring.
Every day Pearl watered her seed.
Every night the moon shined on
the tiny pot.

Until one day two little green leaves
poked through the brown dirt.
Pearl ran to Grandpa. "My apple tree
is growing! Just like yours."

Grandpa winked. "Maybe we'll have
a nice picnic under it this spring."
Pearl smiled. "You're just teasing.
Aren't you?" she asked Grandpa.

Then, early one morning, with the first birds chirping, the yellow sun shining brightly, and the buds bursting through the ground, Pearl and Grandpa dug a hole. Not too deep. Pearl planted her tree. She patted the earth around the sprout. And watered every spot. And smiled.

"Spring, finally," Grandpa sighed.
Grandpa hugged Pearl. Pearl hugged him back.
"Someday maybe you'll bring your children
and their children under this tree. Who knows?"
"Oh, Grandpa," groaned Pearl. And they had a
picnic. Right next to Pearl's tree.

TREE-PLANTING HOLIDAYS

Trees are celebrated in many parts of the world. In the United States the practice of planting trees on a special day was started by J. Sterling Morton in 1872. His effort to bring trees to the grasslands of Nebraska led to the planting of more than a million trees that year and to the establishment of Arbor Day. Arbor Day usually falls in the spring around the end of April, but the date varies greatly throughout the nation.

In Japan, around the end of January or early February, the Japanese celebrate plum blossoms, *ume* (pronounced OO-may), with festivals in parks everywhere, by eating foods and drinking tea made from the fruit of plum trees.

In China, *Chih Shu Chieh* (*Chih* is plant; *shu* is tree; *chieh* is holiday. Pronounced chu-shoo-GEE-eh.) is a tree-planting festival like our Arbor Day. This holiday marks the beginning of spring. Trees are often planted on the graves of family members as a memorial.

April 5 is Arbor Day, *Shikmokil* (*Shik* is planting; *mok* is tree; *il* is day. Pronounced shik-moke-ILL.), in Korea. Tree-planting ceremonies in public parks and school yards take place.

There is also a Tree Fest on November 13 in Tunisia and a Tree-Planting Day in Lesotho, southern Africa, on March 21.

Trees have significance in many religions. In many African cultures they mark the transition from youth to adulthood. Among the Ndembu, the *mudyi* (milk tree) is a symbol of life and is used in marriage ceremonies. In Nepal, on the border between India and China, a young girl is married to a *bel* (small tree) from early childhood. A "marriage tree" is common in southern India as a representation of an ancestor.

TU B'SHVAT

In Jewish custom, a tree is planted when a baby is born. Both are nurtured as they grow. Eventually, branches of the tree can be made into poles to hold up a *chuppa* (canopy), under which the grown child is married, connecting human beings with the earth and the cycle of life. The Torah, the first five books of the Jewish Bible, is often referred to as the Tree of Life.

Tu b'Shvat (pronounced too-bish-VHAT), the New Year of Trees, is the fifteenth day of the Hebrew month Shvat, which falls in winter, usually late January or early February, when trees form fruit, looking ahead toward spring. Seven "fruits" associated with *eretz Yisrael* (the land of Israel)—olives, dates, figs, grapes, pomegranates, wheat, and barley—are eaten at a special Tu b'Shvat seder. Four cups of wine are sipped, just like at the Passover seder. The hardy olive tree casts shade and provides fruit. It is a sign of hope. The date palm is not only strong and beautiful, but its fruit is sweet. The Torah has been linked to the fig tree, a symbol of peace. The pomegranate, a fruit with a tough skin like an orange, reminds us of the physical outside world that hides and protects the inner spiritual world. Wheat and barley are the fruits of the soil; bread is the staff of life.

There are many symbols and *midrashim* (rabbinic stories that give further meaning to biblical texts) that refer to trees, linking Judaism to the environment. A quotation from the medieval Jewish poet Solomon ibn Gabirol of Málaga, Spain, c. 1020–1057, "The world is a tree, and human beings are its fruit," shows the spirit of the holiday and the importance of our being caretakers for all of nature.

An old man was digging and planting a fig tree
when Hadrian, a Roman emperor, passed his path
and asked, "How old are you this day?"
"A hundred years old," the old man answered.
"What are you doing? Don't you know it will be
many years before that tree gives fruit? Do you
ever hope to eat them? You might not be alive."
The old man said, "If I am worthy, I shall eat, and
if not. . . . Those who came before me planted trees.
Shouldn't I do the same for the next generation?"
In the course of time the tree produced figs.
The old man lived long enough to enjoy the fruit
of his labors and brought baskets to the emperor
who honored him.

—Based on the midrash Leviticus Rabbah 25.5

"Even though you will find the land full of good
things, don't say, 'We will sit and not plant.' Rather,
be careful to plant trees. Just as you found trees others
had planted, you should plant for your children.
No one should say, 'I am old. How many more years
will I live? Why should I bother myself for the sake
of others?' Just as you found trees, you should add
more by planting even if you are old."

—Midrash Tanchuma, Kedoshim, after 800 C.E.

How to Grow a Tree

Check with your local nursery to learn which kinds of trees grow best in your area and if you need to prepare your seeds in any way before you plant them. An apple tree like Pearl's must grow for as long as three or as many as seven to ten years before it produces any fruit.

If your soil does not freeze during the winter,
you can plant seeds outside in a sunny spot.
1. Use three large seeds, or several small seeds.
2. Dig a small hole about 4 inches deep.
3. Add 1/4 teaspoon nitrogen fertilizer.
4. Cover it with 3 inches of soil.
5. Place seeds in hole. Cover them with fine soil.
6. Keep soil moist so seeds will germinate.

In a cold climate, plant your seeds in a flowerpot
following the above instructions.
1. Keep flowerpot on a sunny windowsill. Water every day. Wait for seeds to sprout.
2. In spring when the soil thaws, plant seedling outdoors. Dig a hole twice the depth and width of the flowerpot
3. Fill the hole and the flowerpot with water. When the water is drained, gently tap the flowerpot so that the seedling comes out with its soil around it. Loosen a few roots from the bottom of the soil before putting the seedling into the hole.
4. Fill the hole with soil so the tree stands upright. Create a little well around the base.
5. Water the ground around the tree immediately and every day for a week. Then water twice a week. By late spring, the tree will have new growth.

Book designed by Jane Breskin Zalben
The text and display type was set in Bembo.
The illustrations were done on opaline parchment
in watercolor with a series seven triple zero brush.
The endpapers are hand-made from the bark of a fig tree.

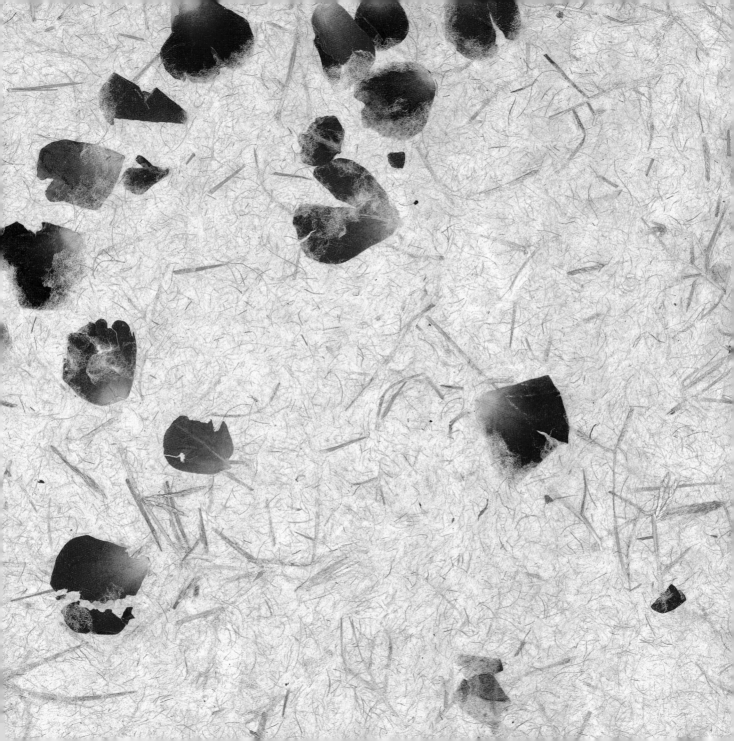

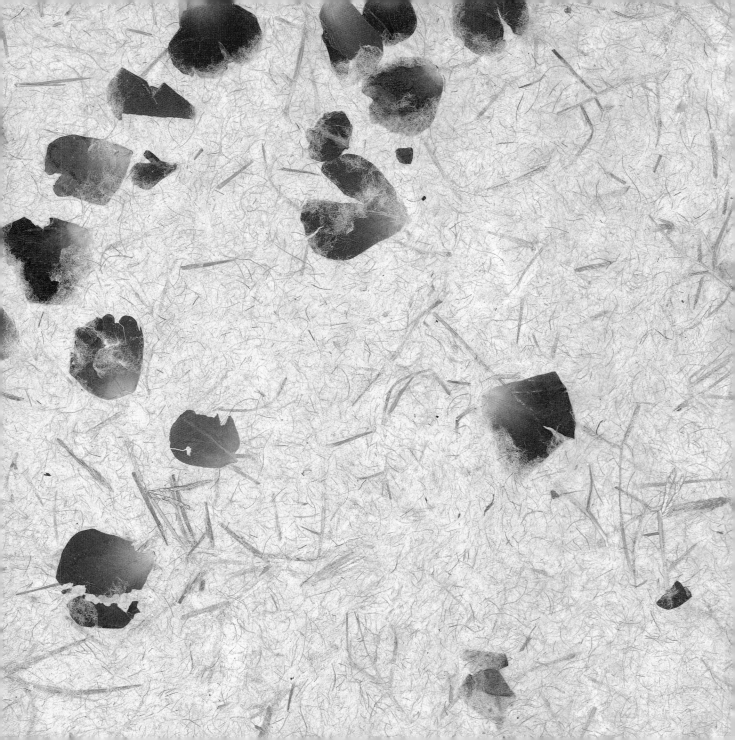